P9-CQE-765

The Adventures of Everyday Geniuses

If You're So Smart, How Come You Can't Spell Mississippi?

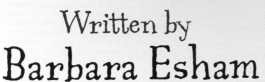

Written by
Barbara Esham

Illustrated by
Mike & Carl Gordon

Published by Mainstream Connections, Perry Hall, MD

ISBN 978-1-60336-448-5 • LCCN 2007908044

My dad is the smartest person I know. He is one of the busiest lawyers in Chicago, and he works hard to keep justice in our city. For the past year my dad has been getting ready for a big case.

Have YOU ever worked on anything for a year?

I'm a third grader at Westover Elementary School.
My name is Katie and I'm only eight, but I've been working
on something too. It's called observation. It's fun because —
let me tell you — I've seen some strange things....

Like the time David, a boy in my class, couldn't resist squeezing the pudding cup that was packed in his lunchbox. He had to see how much pressure the lid could take before...

well, you know....

3

And the time my little sister insisted that our family change her name to Eduardo after she finished watching the Cooking with Eduardo show with Grandma.
My little sister is only three years old.
I guess she thought it was time for a change.

Just last week I saw Mrs. Higgins driving through town with fourteen Chihuahuas in her car... and those were just the Chihuahuas that I could count as she was driving by.
As you can see, observation is a worthwhile pastime.

5

But the strangest thing that I have ever observed happened tonight, while I was practicing for my spelling test.

I asked my dad if he could help me with the toughest word on my spelling list: Mississippi. Usually my dad loves to help me, but this time he said, "I'm not sure. Go ask your mom."

6

"How can you, Daddy, one of the smartest people I know, not know how to spell Mississippi?" I asked in astonishment.

"Well, Katie, I never have been a very good speller. In fact, I don't believe that I have ever spelled Mississippi correctly. Actually there are a lot of words I've never spelled correctly," he answered.

"This is the strangest thing that I have heard of, Daddy, even stranger than Eduardo!" I replied. "How did you make it through the third grade if you couldn't spell Mississippi?"

"Well, it wasn't easy. I was often ashamed of not being able to spell the words on my spelling tests.

In fact, some of my classmates even made fun of me," he said with a serious smile.

"Daddy, do you mean that you were kind of like Mark Twingle? He sits in front of me and he can't spell anything!"

"I guess I was like Mark Twingle," he said. "It's very difficult when you're the kid in the class who works extra hard and still has trouble. I had to spend so much more time on my homework than my sister spent on hers. I would still come home with a C- on my spelling test, and that was on a good day."

"Oooohhhhh, that's terrible," I replied. It was terrible —
and also confusing. I mean, my dad is smart.

"Learning to read was just as difficult," said my dad. "I was the
last kid in my class to learn how to read. Sometimes I would hide
my head when my teacher would ask me to read to the class."

"Just like Mark does!" I shouted.

How could this be?
My dad, just like Mark Twingle?

This doesn't make sense...

"Katie, we have talked about dyslexia before, remember? Dyslexia is a word used to describe the difficulty that some people experience with reading and spelling, like me," he said after looking over my math homework.

"But Daddy, how do you do your job? How can you be so smart if you can't spell or read very well?" I asked.

"Katie, dyslexia does not mean a person isn't smart. In fact, some of the greatest scientists, doctors, and inventors struggled with symptoms of dyslexia," my dad said with a chuckle.

Now, I've observed many strange things, but could it be true that Mark Twingle is the next great mind of our time? Is this possible?

I would need to do a little investigating before I was convinced.

On Saturday, I asked my mom to take me to the public library. I'm a whiz at the library and it didn't take long to find a book about dyslexia.

It included a list of people throughout history who struggled with reading or spelling. But I'm confused. Now that we know about dyslexia, why is this still a secret? Why hasn't anyone ever mentioned it or these folks in school?

17

Like this guy: Dr. John R. Skoyles He works as a neuroscience researcher. Whoa! He researches things I can't even pronounce! Where is the librarian when you need her the most?
One of his book reports is titled, "The Aetioloy of Autism: Neuroembryology and Prefrontal Neocerebellum...." I guess I'll learn about that in fourth grade.

In the meantime, I'll ask some of my friends if they can say "Prefrontal Neocerebellum" three times fast...

I turned the page to read about Archer Martin , a chemist who won the Nobel Prize in 1952. Fortunately the librarian walked by.

"Mrs. Meeks, can you help me read this? Some of the words are a little big," I asked quietly.

"Sure. I love to see children reading on the weekends," she said.

"Let's see here," said Mrs. Meeks. "Archer Martin's experiments include the discovery of a method for detecting pyro-electricity by...

"...observing the attraction of a metal plate of crystals that had been immersed in liquid air. Katie, do you need this information for a book report?" she asked with a puzzled look on her face.

"No, no, Mrs. Meeks, I am just doing a little bit of investigating."

Detecting pyro-electricity in liquid air? Is anyone following me on this one?

"Do you want me to keep reading?" Mrs. Meeks asked.

"Oh yes, please," I replied with my most polite voice. I needed help to get through this book.

"Helen B. Tausig was a doctor in the 1930s. Many women at that time didn't even have a chance to go to college, but Helen Tausig studied to become a pediatric cardiologist. She helped discover a new way to help babies who were born with heart problems. She was the first woman to become a full professor at Johns Hopkins University and she was elected president of the American Heart Association."

"She was really smart!" I said.

"I have to go help some other children now, Katie. Do you think you can take it from here?" asked Mrs. Meeks.

"I'll give it a try," I replied. "If Helen Tausig had trouble reading and writing and she could become a pediatric cardiologist, well I guess I can try to read this book on my own."

Let's see. William James was a psychologist — one of the greatest psychologists of all time. It looks like he had a lot of interesting things to say. A few of them are right here, in this book. Hey, I think Dad has a few of his books at home!

"I don't sing because I am happy, I am happy because I sing."

"Act as if what you do makes a difference. It does."

"Every good worth possessing must be paid for
in strokes of daily effort."

Hey! My dad has this quote framed;
he keeps it on the wall for everyone to notice...

"Do every day or
two something
for no other reason
than its difficulty."

There are so many names in this book...
It would take a long time to read them all...

I guess a lot of people who have trouble with reading and writing go on to become great things: actors, artists, athletes, presidents, doctors, lawyers, writers, scientists, entrepreneurs, inventors, and even teachers.

BOOKS MAKE

I wonder if my teacher, Mrs. Peterson, knows about dyslexia and all these great people... I have a feeling that most of these great people had someone to help them through the tough times, when they might have been feeling frustrated or sad.

Maybe their parents were patient and supported them.

Maybe they had a teacher who could see how smart they were anyway.

Maybe the classmate sitting next to them didn't make them feel badly for not being the fastest reader or the best speller.

21

Now I know why my dad likes what William James
had to say so long ago...

"Do every day or two something
for no other reason than its difficulty."
~William James

Is this what people who struggle with dyslexia
tell themselves each day before school?

Did my dad say this to himself through the tough times, when he was trying his best to learn to read and spell?

I can't wait to go to school on Monday.
I think Mark Twingle needs to know
how great his mind is
and what incredible things he might
accomplish one day...

Maybe, I'm just the right person to tell him.

27

From Dr. Edward Hallowell,

New York Times national best seller, former Harvard Medical School instructor, and current director of the Hallowell Center for Cognitive and Emotional Health...

Fear is the great disabler. Fear is what keeps children from realizing their potential. It needs to be replaced with a feeling of I-know-I-can-make-progress-if-I-keep-trying-and-boy-do-I-ever-want-to-do-that!

One of the great goals of parents, teachers, and coaches should be to find areas in which a child might experience mastery, then make it possible for the child to feel this potent sensation.

The feeling of mastery transforms a child from a reluctant, fearful learner into a self-motivated player.

The mistake that parents, teachers, and coaches often make is that they demand mastery rather than lead children to it by helping them overcome the fear of failure.

The best parents are great teachers. My definition of a great teacher is a person who can lead another person to mastery.

~Dr. Hallowell

To read Dr. Hallowell's full letter, go to our website! Check out what ALL THE OTHER EXPERTS are saying about The Adventures of Everyday Geniuses book series. www.MainstreamConnections.org

A Note to Parents & Teachers

Mainstream Connections would like to help you help your kids become **Everyday Geniuses!**

These fun stories are an easy way to discuss learning styles and obstacles that can impede a child's potential.

The science of learning is making its way into the classroom! Everyday Geniuses are making their debut!

Call, email, or visit the website to learn how YOU can make a difference.

28   All books are available in bulk at discount for qualifying
schools and professional organizations. Contact us!

The Adventures of Everyday Geniuses

RESOURCES for PARENTS and TEACHERS

The BIG LIST of resources can be found on our website. The big list is for parents and teachers, you know, just to give them the latest information on how our brains really learn, and what being smart is all about.

The topic of this book — DYSLEXIA — is a learning obstacle for many Everyday Geniuses. Experts in reading development estimate that one out of every five individuals experience some characteristics of dyslexia!

Mainstream Connections provides you respected resources to help you create a happy, healthy learning environment for every child.

DOWNLOAD your complimentary Resource List today!

WEBSITES
Links to great sites to learn more about learning styles.

BOOK LISTS
Learn more about dyslexia and the science of reading.

CONNECT
News, info & support!

www.MainstreamConnections.org

The Mainstream Connections mission is to expose the broader definitions of learning, creativity, and intelligence. A substantial portion of all profits is held to fund and support the development of programs and services to give all children the tools needed for success.

Are you an EVERYDAY GENIUS TOO?

Get online with your favorite characters from

The Adventures of Everyday Geniuses

There is SO MUCH to do online!

- Meet the Gang and see what they are up to: ideas, inventions and algorithms, poems and other literary works, sEduardo's latest recipe, and get a list of great minds from the past and present!
- Download pages for coloring!
- Hats, Shirts, Classroom Stuff!

www.MainstreamConnections.org

Visit our website to learn more! Adults should always supervise children's web activity.

BOOK INFORMATION

If You're So Smart, How Come You Can't Spell Mississippi
written by Barbara Esham illustrated by Mike & Carl Gordon

Published by Mainstream Connections Publishing
P.O. Box 398, Perry Hall Maryland 21128

Copyright © 2008, Barbara Esham. All rights reserved.

No part of this publication may be reproduced in whole or in part, in any form without permission from the publisher. *The Adventures of Everyday Geniuses* is a registered trademark.

Book design by Pneuma Books, LLC. www.pneumabooks.com

Printed in China ∞ Library Binding

FIRST EDITION

15 14 13 12 11 10 09 08   01 02 03 04 05 06 07 08

JAN 0 / 2014

CATALOGING-IN-PUBLICATION DATA

Esham, Barbara.

If you're so smart, how come you can't spell Mississippi? / written by Barbara Esham ; illustrated by Mike & Carl Gordon. -- 1st ed. -- Perry Hall, MD : Mainstream Connections, 2008.

p. ; cm.

(Adventures of everyday geniuses)

ISBN: 978-1-60336-448-5

Audience: Ages 5-10.

Summary: Introduces the mainstream student and educator to the world of the child who struggles academically. The main character discovers her father is dyslexic, as is one of her classmates-- and she tries to make sense of it. She learns that many successful adults have dyslexia and is inspired to raise awareness about this learning condition.

1. Dyslexic children--Juvenile fiction. 2. Self-esteem--Juvenile fiction. 3. Spelling ability--Juvenile fiction. 4. Anxiety--Juvenile fiction. 5. Learning disabled children--Juvenile fiction. 6. Cognitive styles in children. 7. [Dyslexic children--Fiction. 8. Dyslexia--Fiction. 9. Anxiety--Fiction. 10. Learning disabilities--Fiction.] I. Gordon, Mike. II. Gordon, Carl. III. Title. IV. Series.

PZ7.E74583 .I4 2008   2007908044

[Fic]--dc22   0804

1-14

E   Esham, Barbara
     If you're so smart, how come
you can't spell Mississippi?

For Ben, Sophie, Cooper, Hannah, and all
the others who grow with the special love
that knows no borders.

Special thanks to Lisa Coker, Cumoron
and Hannah's mom, and Namyi Min,
Spence-Chapin Services.

Library of Congress Cataloging-in-Publication Data ✳ Heo, Yumi. ✳ Ten days and nine nights / Yumi Heo. — 1st ed. ✳ p. cm.
Summary: A young girl eagerly awaits the arrival of her newly-adopted sister from Korea, while her whole family prepares.
ISBN 978-0-375-84718-9 (hardcover) — ISBN 978-0-375-94715-5 (Gibraltar lib. bdg.)
[1. Adoption—Fiction. 2. Sisters—Fiction. 3. Family life—Fiction. 4. Korean Americans—Fiction.] ✳ I. Title.
PZ7.H4117Ten 2009 ✳ [E]—dc22 ✳ 2007044073

The text of this book is set in Tyrnavia.
The illustrations are rendered in oil, pencil, and collage on 140-pound Fabriano paper.

MANUFACTURED IN MALAYSIA ✳ 10 9 8 7 6 5 4 3 2 1 ✳ May 2009 ✳ First Edition

ten days
and nine nights

an adoption story by
yumi heo

schwartz & wade books · new york

I mark a circle on the calendar.

I have ten days
and nine nights.

Daddy and I say goodbye to Mommy.

I have nine days
and eight nights.

I make a drawing of my kitty and cut
a heart shape from red paper.

I have eight days
and seven nights.

Grandpa redecorates my room.

I have seven days
and six nights.

I practice.

I have six days
and five nights.

Daddy buys some new furniture.

I have five days
and four nights.

I wash my old teddy bear.

I have four days
and three nights.

Grandma makes a little pink dress.

I have three days
and two nights.

I tell Molly.

I have two days
and one night.

Daddy puts the CLOSED sign
on his dry cleaning store.

I have only
one day!

At last!

I have no days
and no nights.

I have a new baby sister.

author's note

The first time I met a child who had been adopted from Korea—where I was born and lived until I was twenty-four years old—was eighteen years ago on a ski trip to Massachusetts. I was cautiously learning to step with my long skis, and he was my teenage instructor. It was strange to see someone from my country who was so adept at a Western sport, but it also made me feel proud of him. He had come such a long way, without his birth parents, and was thriving. Over the years, as I settled in the suburbs and raised my own family, I ran into Asian—and particularly Korean—adoptees more often. When my son was in preschool, the parents of his best friend, Cameron, adopted a little girl, Hannah, from Korea. My neighbor's good friends' children were adopted from Korea; now they are in college. My friends Shirley and David adopted their three children from Cambodia. For years, Ben, their first child, thought babies came from airplanes! As a Korean who adopted the United States as my home, I've always felt a kinship with these children. I wanted to create a story especially for them and their new families.

a few facts: The number of children adopted from other countries increases every year in the United States. In Korea, before children are adopted they are usually placed in foster homes. Most countries that allow international adoption place children in group homes or orphanages, but there are some that use foster homes as well.

CW 24   A 7/15/09
LC 9/4/20   TC 24

7-09

E   Heo, Yumi
            Ten days and nine nights.